I'm a Pretty Princess

This book is dedicated to every little girl
who needs to find her inner princess.

This book is for

_____

Always remember that you are a pretty

princess!

My name is Makayla and I'm a princess

I wear high heeled shoes and a pink and blue dress

I have a tiara I wear on my head

I like it so much that I wear it to bed

I have my own wand and it shines oh so bright

You can still see it after you turn off the light

We live in a castle that's far, far away

In a land where rainbow-colored unicorns play

The King is my father, the Queen is my mother

Prince Alexander is my little brother

Mommy and Daddy both have sparkly crowns
Daddy wears a red cape, mommy wears fancy gowns

Our family pictures are up on the wall

I like looking at them when I skate down the hall

I have a pet goldfish I call Mister Blue
He's the king of the sea so he wears a crown too

Tea parties are fun with Ciara and Bree
We eat strawberry cupcakes and drink fancy tea

To be a good princess there are things I must do

I must be kind to others

Say please

And thank you

Clean up my room if I make a big mess

Put away my toys and hang up my dress

When I finish my list at the end of the day
I'm really proud that I can say
It's not my castle, my wand, or the dress that I'm in
What makes me a princess is what lies within

So even if you don't have a crown
A wand, a big castle, or a long fancy gown

I bet if you look in the mirror too
You'll see a pretty princess looking right back at you

The End

Made in the USA
Middletown, DE
30 May 2021